E 3086

MW00748104

SEP - - 2009 **DATE DUE**

Bow-Wow! Peep!

Bow-Wow! Peep!

Copyright © 2006
Dalmatian Press, LLC

The DALMATIAN PRESS name is a trademark
of Dalmatian Press, LLC, Franklin, Tennessee 37067.
No part of this book may be reproduced or copied in any form
without the written permission of Dalmatian Press.
Design by Dan Waters

ISBN: 1-40372-351-6
13307

06 07 08 09 WAI 10 9 8 7 6 5 4 3 2 1

Bow-Wow! Peep!

by Kathryn Knight

Illustrated by Bridget Starr Taylor

Dalmatian 🐾 Press

Big Pal. Small Pal. Bow-wow! Peep!

Short pal. Tall pal. Quack-quack! Humm...

Curly tail. Long tail. Oink-oink! Squeak!

Hoofy feet. Webby feet. Moo-moo! Honk!

Woolly hair. Straight hair. Baa-baa! Meow!

Tiny hands. Fluffy wings. Chee-chee! Cluck!

Gray hair. Green skin. Hee-haw! Ribbit!

White tail. Red tail. Neigh! Doodle-doo!

Short horns. Long ears. Naa-naa! Sniff!

Big, small. Short, tall.

Different? Yes! But pals all!

Buzzz-buzzz! Wink!